MW01602136

About the Author

Robert Berger has an A.S. in Environmental Science, a Paralegal Certificate and spent his career working in the healthcare field for Yale University School of Medicine, Yale-New Haven Hospital and Bristol-Myers Squibb. A lifelong resident of Connecticut, Robert writes fictional tales based on experience and in his free time he enjoys playing cribbage, sipping margaritas and driving a little too fast in his sporty coupe… but not necessarily in that order.

Nerves of Steele

Robert Berger

Nerves of Steele

Olympia Publishers
London

www.olympiapublishers.com
OLYMPIA PAPERBACK EDITION

Copyright © Robert Berger 2022

The right of Robert Berger to be identified as author of
this work has been asserted in accordance with sections 77 and 78 of
the Copyright, Designs and Patents Act 1988.

All Rights Reserved

No reproduction, copy or transmission of this publication
may be made without written permission.
No paragraph of this publication may be reproduced,
copied or transmitted save with the written permission of the publisher,
or in accordance with the provisions
of the Copyright Act 1956 (as amended).

Any person who commits any unauthorised act in relation to
this publication may be liable to criminal
prosecution and civil claims for damage.

A CIP catalogue record for this title is
available from the British Library.

ISBN: 978-1-80074-898-9

This is a work of fiction.
Names, characters, places and incidents originate from the writer's
imagination. Any resemblance to actual persons, living or dead, is
purely coincidental.

First Published in 2022

Olympia Publishers
Tallis House
2 Tallis Street
London
EC4Y 0AB

Printed in Great Britain

Dedication

To my sister, Barbara, who passed far too young from Huntington's disease.

Acknowledgements

I would like to acknowledge the extraordinary support I received from Sharon 'Stone Cold' Cullen who encouraged me to keep writing even after I got buried under a mountain's worth of rejection emails for ten years. This work never would've been published without the sharp, editorial eye of Katie Murphy who reviewed the first draft... and rightly dropped the hammer on me—I'm glad she did. There were glaring issues with structure and style, and without a swift kick in the backside the story would still be sitting on my laptop, never to see the publishing light of day.

I'd like to give special thanks to old friend Michael Marsland who took the cover photograph of yours truly. Mike graciously donated his skills and time doing the best he could to make me look presentable, which is no easy task.

Dylan Steele's personal life was more off-kilter than his golf game and the man who wanted to settle down and start a family couldn't find Ms Right, but not for lack of trying. Dylan signed up with dating websites, dated a few co-workers or went on blind dates but nothing ever clicked and he began to doubt if he'd ever find his soulmate.

At least Dylan's professional life moved in the right direction; he graduated from Wesleyan University with a B.A. in Accounting and minored in American Literature, never losing his love for the written word. Dylan worked for Coopers and Lybrand, a Big Eight accounting firm with offices located in the small port city of New Haven, Connecticut and only a ten-mile commute from his hometown of Branford.

Dylan had a sweeping view of New Haven's sprawling harbor from his fourth-floor office in the Long Wharf Maritime Center and on a clear day he could see the glittering sand dunes on Long Island's north shore. Taking a break from debits and credits for a few minutes, Dylan sipped a steaming cup of Italian Roast and gazed out a window admiring the stark, Ansel Adams beauty of a wintry, December day.

While scanning the distant horizon, Dylan could've sworn he saw a mermaid splashing about in the harbor's shallow, gray waters but wrote it off as nothing more than his mind playing tricks on him because he'd been putting in long days and was exhausted.

Eight hours later, Dylan poured three fingers of Jack Daniel's and plopped down on his living room couch to watch the evening news. Stories about pockets of anarchy sprouting up like toadstools all over the world, celebutantes involved in Twitter spats or politicians spewing venom about their rivals dominated today's headlines, just like every other day.

With planet Earth inching toward total annihilation, Dylan went into the kitchen to prepare what might be his last supper and thought his mind played tricks on him again because he couldn't help but notice the hands on a wall clock were spinning backwards and then the timepiece melted like a Salvador Dalí painting.

It was Christmas time but Dylan didn't have visions of sugar plums dancing in his head; nope, cavorting mermaids and melting clocks did the tango there, and the music wouldn't stop. There's nothing more frightening than the unknown and Dylan felt real fear for the first time in his life, certain he'd lost his sanity without knowing why. Dylan called for medical assistance and was whisked away to Shoreline Medical Center where he was poked, prodded and scanned by every gizmo in the arsenal.

Dylan was diagnosed with a rare form of diabetes known as Hyperosmolar Hyperglycemic Nonketotic Syndrome (HHNS) and the hallucinations that accompany this ailment were the least of Dylan's problems: left untreated, death would be knockin' on his door.

Dr Gerald Livingstone was *the* endocrinologist to treat HHNS patients in the New Haven area and he got Dylan back on his feet the next day but Dylan needed weekly, then monthly appointments with Dr Livingstone to ensure Dylan's glucose levels were being regulated properly to prevent Frolicking Mermaid vs. Dissolving Clock: The Sequel.

Terri Pace worked in Livingstone's office as a Physician Associate assigned to assist with Dylan's ongoing needs and she too wanted to settle down with Mr Right and start a family but the men she dated were decidedly Mr Wrong. And then Dylan waltzed into her life.

The air practically crackled with electricity when Dylan and Terri first met as they shared one of those *je ne sais quoi*, instant attractions that only seem to happen in movies or Harlequin romance novels. Terri flirted with Dylan making it clear she wanted to take him out for a test drive and Dylan would never U-turn away from a lady who was easy on the eyes *and* healed the sick at the same time. The two started dating and discovered a mutual passion for the game of golf, Italian food as well as the common bond of growing up and spending their entire lives in Branford. Six months later, Dylan popped the question.

Terri would be a June bride but it wasn't all sunshine and flowers: she was in the unenviable position of coping with Rebecca, Dylan's mother, a woman Terri referred to as 'smother-in-law' as well as many other names never to be repeated in polite society. "For better or worse" was worse with Rebecca and their relationship was chilly, bordering on Arctic, and Terri would have her hands full for years to come.

As Terri's wedding day approached, she hoped Rebecca would be on her best behavior and not throw the most important day of Terri's life into disarray—it's called a pipe dream for a reason. Standing up in front of God and everyone at Terri's wedding rehearsal dinner, a tipsy Rebecca gave the last rites to her relationship with Terri after proposing a toast congratulating Dylan on his marriage to "Plan B."

Ten… nine… eight… seven…

Terri had to be restrained by two burly groomsmen before she did something foolish that would prompt an official police investigation as she fantasized about how to eliminate Rebecca from the human gene pool in the most gruesome way possible and not end up in the slammer—abandoned building… down a flight of stairs… into a drum of acid. Terri wisely set aside her rage for the moment and chose not to commit murder because she didn't want to spend her wedding day being interrogated by hard-boiled detectives asking probing questions: where was Terri when Rebecca got whacked and what about that receipt for a 55-gallon drum of sulfuric acid? After Dylan had a little *conversation* with mom, the wedding went off without a hitch.

Like so many women, Rebecca outlived her man and was widowed far too young at age sixty-four. Rebecca's husband was her rock, her anchor and she didn't handle his passing well; there's only one thing worse than being widowed—being widowed and lonely—and Rebecca had to fend for herself for the first time in over thirty years.

Rebecca didn't have many friends and had a brother who shared the same prickly genetics but he irritated people

on the left coast in La Jolla, California. All Rebecca had was one family lifeline: her only child and, guilt by association, Terri. It finally dawned on Rebecca that she needed to play nice with others or she'd spend her golden years all by her lonesome and she reached out to Terri seeking to mend fences but turning over a new leaf proved to be a challenge.

Rebecca's attempts to make amends were well-intentioned and Terri knew having a civil relationship with Rebecca was best for all concerned so Terri was willing to bury the hatchet instead of planting it in the middle of Rebecca's forehead.

Rebecca still gummed-up the works by making it clear she wanted to hear the pitter-patter of grandchildren feet sooner rather than later. With the subtlety of someone screaming "Bomb!" in a crowded building, Rebecca dropped hints that Terri needed to start a family today—not tomorrow or next month—because Terri's egg timer was running out of sand and you can't turn back the hands of time.

Six… five… four… three…

Terri and Dylan lived in a cozy, waterfront sanctuary called Granite Bay, a cul-de-sac of sorts with slender ribbons of asphalt crisscrossing and spider-webbing off Grove Street, the main artery snaking through this slice of coastal paradise. At least residents could enjoy the view because Granite Bay's beach is called 'Scum Beach,' a mucky, muddy tidal flat at anything but the highest of high tides.

Terri was pleasantly surprised that for the most part Rebecca was on her best behavior but all good things come to an end eventually and Terri had no one to blame but

herself by giving Rebecca what she wanted the most—a grandson. So much for best behavior: a doting, hovering grandmother loomed in Terri's future.

Samuel Steele made a memorable entrance into this world coming to life two weeks earlier than planned and he was in a big hurry: soon after waking up one morning Terri went into labor and twenty-three minutes later Sam announced his arrival as Terri screeched unholy sounds that would frighten The Grim Reaper.

Dylan winced at the disturbing sight of watery fluid and an assortment of gross, disgusting discharges flowing out of Terri's body like a raging river and moments later Sam somersaulted to life like an Olympic gymnast... and he even stuck the landing. After all was said and done, mother and son survived the ordeal only slightly worse for the wear; Dylan not so much. A changed man scarred for life after witnessing the horrifying miracle of birth, Dylan never, ever wanted to experience amniotic fluid, placentas or umbilical cords again.

As the days and weeks sailed past, there were more than a few testy moments between Rebecca and Terri because an all-knowing grandma shared her infinite knowledge of parenting wisdom with Terri whether Terri wanted to hear it or not. There were one too many Queen Bees in this hive and tensions started to rise; it was only a matter of time before Terri lured Rebecca to an abandoned building giving grandma an ultimatum: stairs, drum and death or back off, be quiet and continue breathing.

A simmering feud came to a full, rolling boil when Rebecca noted that Dylan didn't seem to be his usual happy-go-lucky self lately. Rebecca should've just gone

ahead and challenged Terri to pistols at noon because grandma pointed an accusatory finger at Terri suggesting the unthinkable: Dylan's spirits were low because Terri wasn't woman enough to keep her man satisfied.

Two... one... zero... we have liftoff...

Dylan was in the middle of shaving but almost sliced open a jugular when Terri startled him after stampeding into the bathroom like a spooked Holstein and, almost vibrating with anger, Terri could barely speak:

"Rainy day fund... ten grand... hitman to off Rebecca... today would be good."

"Ten thou? That's a bit pricey, don't you think? You'd take Mom out for a Dr Pepper and Eskimo Pie."

"Now is not the time... her corpse, your corpse... at this point it doesn't make any difference; I'll get the chair either way."

"What did she do now?"

"Rebecca believes you're not getting enough; what do you think?"

Giving Dylan no time to answer, Terri strongly suggested that he choose his next words carefully or they'd be the last ones he'd ever speak. Dylan wisely avoided answering the loaded question and instead convened a family summit to clear the air. The meeting was more like an exorcism and after Rebecca's demons were cast off, strict rules curbing her worst instincts were established— cease and desist with the hovering and smothering, and if Terri wants advice, she'll ask for it.

Rebecca finally got the message and took a gentler approach to grandmother-ing, and two years later Terri gave birth to Amy. Unlike her older brother, Amy made a grand entrance into the world when she damn well felt like forcing Mom to suffer the aches, pains and torment of a 24-hour labor. This time Terri kept the screaming to a minimum by opting for an epidural and delivered Amy from the safety of a Neonatal Intensive Care Unit; even better Dylan observed Amy's birth from far, far away... on television from a nearby room for those too squeamish to experience the wonder of childbirth in person.

It was a glorious Saturday morning that held so much promise—the sun shone, birds chirped, and lawn mowers mowed—because Terri and Dylan planned on spending a family day at the beach building sandcastles, grilling hot dogs and hamburgers, and keeping the kids slathered in SPF 50 sunblock to prevent them from looking like cooked lobsters by the end of the day.

Terri prepared a breakfast of scrambled eggs with a side of sausage and chomped down on a hardened chunk of some God-knows-what, meat-like byproduct that cracked a molar. In absolute agony, Terri needed repair but she had a phobia about dentists and even getting a routine cleaning sent her running for the exit in need of a straightjacket and forced sedation.

Terri almost had a cow when she learned the one and only dentist she trusted was on vacation and any emergencies that arose were handled by a colleague, Dr Roger Mason. The very last thing Terri wanted was having an unfamiliar, wild-eyed oral surgeon rummaging around in her mouth, poking and prodding her with power drills and pointy-sharp instruments but she had no choice.

Dr Mason wasn't the Angel of Death and greeted Terri with a smile and promise to ease her pain as quickly as possible. In order to determine the extent of the damage, Mason used a panoramic x-ray machine to take a 360-degree scan of Terri's mouth and the equipment looked like it came straight out of a James Bond movie, something Q would give 007 to help thwart evil people from becoming King of the World.

Already on the verge of losing control, Terri didn't react well to being tethered to the porta-potty-sized contraption that had *Radiation Hazard* prominently displayed in six-inch high, bright red letters across the top. That's the very, very last thing Terri needed to see as Mason wrapped Velcro straps around Terri's wrists, ankles, forehead and neck lashing her to a device that would make Rube Goldberg proud. Terri was concerned that after undergoing the DNA-altering scan, she'd mutate into a ten-legged creature that just slithered out of the primordial ooze, but her fears were unfounded and she survived wholly intact.

The tooth needed to be removed and Dr Mason wisely used nitrous oxide as an anesthetic to prevent Terri from jumping out of the chair and running from the building like it was on fire. A little dazed and unsteady on her feet, Terri emerged from the surgical suite sans one tooth but no longer in pain and thought this day couldn't possibly get any worse—those famous last words will haunt you every time.

After Terri arrived home, Dylan wryly observed that she looked all right and, in all likelihood, would make a full recovery but his foray into stand-up comedy fell flat and thudded to earth in lead balloon fashion. Terri filed that comment away for future reference; it's a bad idea to annoy a lady who forgets nothing and gleefully exacts a pound of flesh from anyone foolish enough to get on her bad side.

A day at the beach was postponed and the long day finally came to an end with Terri looking forward to getting a good night's sleep hoping Sunday would be devoid of medical emergencies, but that was another pipe dream. Terri dozed off thinking about the good ol' days *waaaay* back this morning when she had a full complement of teeth and then reality rudely interrupted when out of the blue Dylan's nose began bleeding… and bleeding… and bleeding.

Terri did her best to get the nosebleed under control and it's a good thing she never flinched handling bodily fluids because this was particularly bad; she called for an ambulance and moments later EMTs whisked Dylan away—again—to Shoreline Medical Center.

Traumatized at seeing their blood-soaked father hauled away on a stretcher, Terri calmed her children down explaining that even though Dad resembled a victim in a slasher movie, the problem was minor and Dylan would be just fine. Terri knew that was a load of crapola because it doesn't get much worse than a hemorrhaging diabetic and she made a beeline to the Center hoping her betrothed would still be breathing by the time she arrived.

It took about thirty minutes for Dylan's nose to stop leaking a river of blood and as it turned out the nosebleed had nothing to do with diabetes, just one of those random events where the human body reminds us of how frail we are and that life can end suddenly, without warning. When the Steele family was finally allowed to see Dylan, he was slumped over in a chair, weakened from blood loss and sported the oh-so-appealing look of a pallid cadaver. The kids ran into Dylan's arms thrilled that Dad remained among the living and Terri also breathed a huge sigh of relief that Dylan wouldn't be buried six feet deep into terra firma.

Terri's penchant for paying people back ten times over who had the unmitigated gall to cross swords with her bubbled to the surface and she got even with Dylan—and then some—for his wiseass comment about her missing molar.

"You look all right and, in all likelihood, you'll make a full recovery," Terri noted with an evil little grin.

"Amusing, and yes, touché; I deserved that. Can we leave now?"

"Wait; I just got a text from the editor-in-chief of *Zombie Magazine* who wants to put you on the cover of next month's issue."

"I've always admired your empathy and charming compassion."

"I do my best but wow… I've seen some pasty-looking people in my life, but you… wow."

"Again, very amusing. Let's go home, OK?"

"Let's go kids," Terri said as she herded Sam and Amy toward the exit. "Mommy has to drive Daddy home and take care of him… take care of him in ways he never imagined were possible."

Juggling a job, two children, a house and a comedian for a husband didn't leave Terri with much time to do the things she liked: get a round of golf in periodically but, just as important, fill a china closet with antique, ceramic treasures. Terri collected Meissen porcelain dinner ware after getting infected by the Meissen bug when she purchased a nice example for five dollars that was worth over five hundred because the person who sold the piece didn't know Meissen from floor tiles.

Terri would go to great lengths in her quest for ornately decorated plates and bowls, and read an article about Olde Ways, an antique store specializing in Meissen ware. Located half a stone's throw from the Massachusetts state line, Olde Ways would normally be a ninety-minute drive from Branford for cautious, courteous drivers, but only took seventy minutes with lead-foot Terri behind the wheel.

As Terri meandered through a horse barn converted to an antique store, she came across a bowl she'd been seeking for quite some time, the final piece of a matching set. The list price was $150, a little on the high side: the bowl should sell for approximately $125 and Terri haggled with the owner for a lower price, firing off the opening salvo:

"You're killing me... $100."

"I wouldn't sell it to my dying grandmother for that price... $140."

"At the rate you're going, you won't have any customers *or* family left... $110."

"For that price, I wouldn't sell it to my dying mother either... $130."

"How many relatives are you willing to sacrifice? Plus, I've got a kid in college... $115."

"As many as it takes, a kid in college doesn't count plus you drive a $75,000 BMW M4… $125; take it or leave it."

"Point taken… sold."

Terri paid for the bowl with a credit card but the owner came back moments later saying the card got rejected because it was over the limit. No way, Terri thought, I paid off the balance three weeks ago and haven't used it since; the company must've made a mistake. Terri only carried one credit card but she always had two one-hundred-dollar bills in her wallet in case of emergencies and this definitely constituted an emergency; Terri paid cash for the bowl and went home focused on getting answers.

Terri managed to make the journey without Johnny Law pulling her over for reckless driving or speeding—this time anyway—and noticed two letters sitting on the kitchen table addressed to her: one from Kay's Jewelers and the other from a credit union in Colorado both thanking Terri for her business and applying for a mortgage, respectively. Terri never shopped at Kay's or applied for a loan with a company in Colorado and she had that sinking feeling after realizing what happened: her identity was stolen and a thief went on a shopping spree with her credit card as well as purchasing jewelry or trying to buy a house in her name.

It only got worse the next day when Verizon Wireless, a service Terri didn't use, also thanked Terri for her business after a poser purchased five new phones with multiyear service agreements. Terri spent days sending dozens of emails, making phone calls and swearing a blue streak trying to clear up the mess; identity theft is cruel, unfair and capricious: once an identity is stolen, it's stolen for life, sold back and forth among bad people with bad intentions living in extradition-free countries with odd-sounding names like Framistan or Uvanna.

Terri went to Branford Police headquarters to report the crime believing the police would actually do their job and investigate but she was mistaken. Terri met with Officer Mattson to discuss the particulars but he had no interest in hearing Terri's tale of woe; nope, not even a little. He paid Terri no never mind tapping his feet like he had somewhere else to be and handed her a form with a Branford Police Department case number handwritten on it telling Terri to refer to that number if she had any future problems.

When it became clear Mattson had no intention of investigating the crime of the century, Terri stormed off telling Mattson he was more Keystone Cop than Kojak and urged him to turn in his badge. Eventually, the police and the Federal Bureau of Investigation (FBI) did their job taking down a group of criminals who ruined peoples' lives and didn't think twice about it.

Terri's financial life began to unravel because the Accounting Manager at her place of employment developed a bad gambling habit and got in too deep with the wrong people—people who knew guys who knew other guys who took care of things, lots of things. Logan Larrimore didn't want to end up as fish food at the bottom of Long Island Sound and paid off his gambling debt by selling personal information to sketchy types who ran a sophisticated identity theft ring that had worldwide reach.

Logan also paid down the debt by relieving wealthy homes of valuables and then fencing the items to even sketchier types but the police got wind of Logan's wicked ways and placed him under arrest. Stone-faced officers escorted light-fingered Logan to a holding cell to enjoy the company of reasonable, thoughtful fellows nicknamed 'Killer' or 'Psycho' but Logan was having none of that.

Breaking the record for ratting out his colleagues in the shortest time ever, Logan saved his worthless hide by requesting immunity from prosecution and, ironically enough, a new identity in the Witness Protection program for spilling the beans about the entire operation.

Because the identity theft ring had national and international implications, the FBI swooped in to take over the case. The FBI is nothing if not thorough and it took some time to build a rock-solid case; one year later, FBI agents perp-walked dozens of digital pickpockets in front of television cameras for the entire world to see but none were located in Framistan or Uvanna.

It's a good thing the FBI discovered the thieves' lair before Terri found them and meted out her own form of justice by taking the miscreants on a 100 mile-per-hour jaunt down Interstate 95 while tied to the rear bumper of her M4 until their limp, lifeless bodies resembled grated cheese.

As the years piled up, people pretending to be Terri applied for car loans, store credit cards or attempted to hack into the real Terri's bank accounts because identity theft is like herpes: it keeps coming back, over and over again— there is no end and Terri had no choice but to live with it.

Juggling a job, two children, a house and a revenge-minded wife didn't leave much time for Dylan's hobbies either: golf, of course, but, just as important, his love of writing. Even though Dylan worked nine-to-five as a cold, calculating accountant, in the depths of his soul he was an artist who painted with words but Dylan also liked food in the pantry and wasn't about to play the role of starving artiste suffering for his craft; hence the artistic sacrifice of working for a living.

Dylan had two fictional stories published in literary journals but the words that easily tumbled out of his brain onto the page suddenly disappeared into the abyss of writer's block—poof! just gone into the misty ether, perhaps never to return again.

Even though The Blockage lingered and lingered, Dylan never gave up and was determined to write the Great American Novel somehow, some way. He'd position his nimble digits over a laptop's keyboard ready to start tap-tap-tapping away but all Dylan saw was a cursor blinking on and off, mocking him—come on buddy; write a letter, write your congressman, write anything, I dare ya'—but page one remained emptier than a supermarket's shelves just before a hurricane crashes onshore.

Dylan searched The Google to learn how authors broke through the logjam to refill their vacant minds with *Webster* or *Roget*. Remedies such as meditation, holistic massages or smudging a home with sage and lavender were too far-fetched and hippie-dippy for Dylan's tastes, and he homed in on a dietary solution, which made more sense to him.

Many authors claimed that a smoothie made from kale, spinach and cabbage was a magic elixir that cured their writing disease and, desperate to regain his form, Dylan gave it a whirl. As Terri prepared school lunches for the kids one morning, Dylan pureed a foul witch's brew of ripe, stinky plant life that could pass for eye-of-newt and toe-of-frog soup and the nose-holding aroma wafted through the kitchen.

"Oh my God, Dylan; what's that stench... eau de Water Buffalo?" Terri asked as she opened windows to air out the room. "The kitchen smells like a waste treatment plant at low tide."

"I was thinking more elephant than water buffalo and rotting garbage on a 110-degree day."

"Tread lightly, *Mr Steele*... I think the entire house has to be fumigated; nice going."

Uh oh, Dylan thought, nothing good ever happens after Terri refers to me as 'Mr Steele' as he recalled the time Mr Steele spent two weeks in Mansion Bow-Wow after forgetting to shower Terri with gifts on her birthday—and Dylan didn't want to consider the scorched earth Terri would leave in her wake if he forgot their wedding anniversary.

With more than a hint of irritation in her voice, Terri asked Dylan what possessed him to whip up the rancid, emerald-green concoction and he reiterated the dubious claim that micro-nutrients unclog neural pathways and unleash a burst of creative energy the likes of which are beyond comprehension. Terri snorted her contempt for such foolishness and warned Dylan that guzzling toxic waste would unclog more than his brain and she didn't want to reside in the same hemisphere if that happened.

"Perhaps you should consider chugging vodka instead of laxative biohazards," Terri suggested as she poured the smoothie down the drain.

"But I don't like vodka."

"Fair enough; Jack Daniel's then."

"I'm listening."

"It's simple, really: smoothie-bourbon... divorced-not divorced. Have I made myself clear?"

Terri urged Dylan to write a story based on his woefully misguided youth and took a moment to recap an ill-advised escapade Dylan engineered on All Hallows' Eve. Handing Dylan a story title—*The Mischief Night War*—Terri urged Dylan to write a tale about him and his reprobate friends paying the price for destroying personal property the night before Halloween.

Sometimes all that's needed is a nudge... mixed with a shot or two of sour-mash clarity. Dylan loved the idea and with a renewed sense of purpose grabbed his laptop and furiously typed away, his fingers flying across the keyboard at the speed of thought using fake names to protect the guilty...

Donald and Sonia Taylor lived the stress-free life of double income and no children, and had absolutely no desire whatsoever—zero, nada, zilch—to increase Earth's human population. They believed the only good children were silent *and* invisible, and didn't go ga-ga in the presence of little babies, scooping them up to make twisty-strange faces at the squirming bundles of joy.

Nope, Donald and Sonia wanted nothing to do with little people until they became big people—big people who just graduated from college and moved far away from home, but even then, well, the jury was still out. Not surprisingly, the Taylors were no fans of little people begging for candy and didn't participate in the annual event known as Halloween.

Big mistake.

Three pre-teen boys—Kevin, the ringleader of this adolescent circus, his best friend Rex and another boy named Tommy—referred to themselves as Delta Squad One (DS1) and the trio of troublemaking marauders ensured that any neighbors who failed to give out sweet treats on Halloween were taught a lesson on Mischief Night the following year. The boys would add decorative touches to a home's exterior with a coating of raw eggs and toilet paper, and all the king's horses and all the king's men couldn't put smashed pumpkins back together again after DS1 got through with them, leaving the remains on front doorsteps as payback for not toeing the Halloween line.

Nighttime comes early on the 30th of October and after dinner Kevin asked Mom if he could play video games at Tommy's house but that was a lie: Kevin planned on rendezvousing with the other members of DS1 to storm the beaches and launch a ground assault against the Taylor property.

Mom gave Kevin her blessing and on a nearly cloudless night the commandos approached the Taylors' home. Just in the nick of time the moon ducked behind a bank of clouds providing a dense blanket of black to cover a stealthy sneak attack and the boys crawled on their bellies toward the driveway where the Taylors' cars were parked. With laser-guided precision, DS1 bombarded the defenseless vehicles with two dozen eggs while lobbing squeezably-soft hand grenades onto pine trees and then retreated, melting into the darkness before their misdeeds were discovered.

When Donald left for work early the next morning, he saw the messy results of DS1's beach landing and vowed revenge, biding his time for the next 365 days to turn the tables on the scoundrels who ruined two cars and adorned towering evergreens with bathroom tissue.

Donald installed an elaborate security system complete with night vision cameras, digital trip wires and bright flood lights, and when Mischief Night rolled around the following year, Donald put the plan into motion—lure DS1 into a trap and get sweet revenge. Sonia was a head-turner whose singular good looks would make Hollywood starlets green with envy and the plan was to use her feminine charms to draw DS1 into a bottleneck where Donald would be waiting to spring an unpleasant surprise on the lads.

The Taylors' home was completely dark except for a solitary light in the bedroom and the security system alerted Donald when DS1 breached the property. Kevin and his band of brothers were drawn to the light because they could see Sonia standing just inside, faintly silhouetted against a table lamp. She strutted her stuff in a barely-there, sheer negligee that left absolutely nothing to the imagination and, giggling and elbowing each other, DS1 drew closer to get a gander at a lady who was all woman and nothing but woman.

Men of any age never learn; in their zeal to witness flesh and blood beauty in the flesh for the first time in their lives, the boys inadvertently boxed themselves in: with a house on one side and eight-foot-high hedgerows on two others, DS1 had nowhere to run. Donald flipped a switch and five floodlights lit up the yard as he emerged from a hiding place behind a tall oak tree and approached the boys brandishing a shotgun… it wasn't loaded.

Growling like an angry mama bear protecting her cubs, Donald urged DS1 to leave immediately or in quick succession he would: 1) fill them full of lead; 2) set them on fire; and 3) dispose of the burning embers in a contaminated landfill. The boys ran away as fast as their sneakers could carry them and reported the incident to their parents but left out inconsequential details such as trespassing or voyeurism; outraged at Donald's behavior, DS1's parents called Branford Five-0 to file an official complaint.

When police questioned Donald about the incident, he showed them video surveillance from his security system that clearly showed DS1 trespassing onto private property and then admiring a scantily clad woman parading around in the privacy of her own home. After discovering their precious children were pathological liars and miniature Peeping Toms, DS1's parents grounded the boys for the rest of their natural lives until they understood that smashing Jack-O-Lanterns, making omelets out of cars and decorating trees with rolls of toilet paper is not the way to make friends and influence people. The Taylors took a gentler approach to Halloween as well and participated in the candy-giving event to prevent any further warmongering.

In lieu of serving time in Juvenile Detention, DS1 was sentenced to be the designated clean-up crew to undo all the damage they caused to homes throughout their neighborhood. The boys learned a hard lesson: removing toilet paper from 60-foot evergreens and cleaning off dried egg parts from painted surfaces is no easy task and DS1 spent the better part of a week climbing ladders and hosing off houses before being paroled.

The end of hostilities brought peace and prosperity across the land and the area's residents could return to their normal lives no longer worried about roving gangs of punks destroying cars and littering front yards with delicate pieces of paper.

And then there was great rejoicing...

Dylan slumped back in his chair feeling the weight of the world lift off his shoulders. Dylan never suffered from a bout of writer's block again and he was back, badder than ever, banging away on his laptop's keyboard; the Great American Novel was once again within reach.

Located in Branford on the shores of Long Island Sound, Pine Orchard Yacht and Country Club sponsored a golf tournament supporting local charities and Dylan relished the opportunity to play a round at his old stomping grounds, despite the cringe-worthy memories of his youth. When Dylan was thirteen years old, he worked there as a caddie and that experience stayed with him for life, like a piece of bubble gum permanently stuck to the sole of a shoe.

The privileged few with more money than common sense paid top dollar to play eighteen on a perfectly manicured golf course and then sip cocktails on three-masted schooners or ninety-foot Sea Rays moored in the mirror-smooth waters of the Club's private marina. Dylan's family wasn't well off and working at Pine Orchard Club would expose him to wealth the likes of which he'd never experienced before from people for which money was no object, no object at all.

Caddies weren't employees of the club and were treated no better than convicts, forced to schlep forty pounds of dead weight in blazing summer heat for menial wages and no training was provided: new caddies had to learn on the fly and many young men washed out, unable to handle the rigors of the job. After lugging golf clubs around in sweltering, 90-degree temperatures for five hours, players settled up with caddies paying them the whopping sum of five dollars, the flat rate human pack animals were paid after serving out their sentence of hard labor.

The General, The Worm Assassin and The Cheapskate were players caddies avoided like last week's sushi but Dylan couldn't escape the worst of the lot: James McShane, aka The Potty Mouth. Every August Pine Orchard Club sponsored a member-guest tournament and Dylan was handed the frightening assignment of carrying McShane's bag for the day.

McShane was a trust fund baby who stood on the precipice of eternal damnation and didn't care; nope, not one little bit. McShane took the Lord's name in vain whenever the spirit moved him, sprinkling in a few priest and nun jokes along the way. Rounding out McShane's foursome were equally foul-mouthed fellows who did everything they could to join McShane in Hades and behaved worse than children, helicoptering clubs through the air, throwing in a temper tantrum or two.

The group finished the front nine around noon and decided to take a 15-minute, quick-like-a-bunny lunch break to recharge the batteries. However, the pace of lunch more resembled that of a tortoise and the short respite stretched into a two-hour, four-martini bender. The group staggered to the tee believing large quantities of gin made them better golfers but it just made them more profane and even more obnoxious.

McShane was the first to tee off and, almost coming out of his shoes, took a mighty swing that never touched the ball and he came oh so close to keeling over. He stood motionless for a moment and cemented his place in Hell by directing choice comments toward a certain deity, much to the delight of his playing partners who joined the fray making off-color remarks of their own.

The air was filled with salty language and crude asides about the women in attendance as the classy group of guys helicoptered their way through a horrendous round of golf until the caddies were put out of their misery after McShane sank the final putt of the day as the sun started to set.

Dylan couldn't believe the antics McShane and His Disciples engaged in, and the people Dylan thought were a cut above the rest, were anything but; Dylan reached one of those turning points in life and decided to quit the caddie gig because he'd seen enough of how low the upper crust could go and didn't want to see any more.

Fast-forward to the present and Dylan continued his love affair with golf but the feeling wasn't mutual: Dylan did the best he could but the game completely eluded him— simply put, Dylan was a hacker who'd never improve. Terri loved the game just as much as Dylan—the game eluded her as well—but they enjoyed playing together because they'd spend a few hours outdoors on a gorgeous summer day even though their golf game wasn't gorgeous.

Maybe it was the effect of a blue moon or perhaps Dylan's brain transformed into a bowl of oatmeal because when Dylan woke up on the day of the charity event, he inexplicably brimmed with confidence he'd make history and break the 100-stroke barrier for the first time in his life. An azure sky airbrushed with feathery clouds and temperatures in the low 80s would make for a perfect day of golf and Dylan couldn't wait to get the round underway.

Dylan and Terri entered the tournament as a twosome and were paired with another twosome to compete for trophies, prizes and, even more important, bragging rights. The Steeles teamed up with Lorraine and Charlene, two women who headed up one of the charities benefiting from the $250 entry fee, and all participants gathered in the clubhouse to meet their playing partners for the day, sharing pleasantries before the festivities started. Dylan made small talk with Lorraine and innocently posed a question that came out wrong six ways from Sunday. Very few golfers hit it straight down the middle; most shots curve to the left (hook) or to the right (slice) and Dylan asked which direction Lorraine's shots traveled; golden silence would've been preferable.

"So, Lorraine; are you a hooker or sli...?"

Dylan caught himself in mid-sentence but it was too late, the damage was done. As soon as the offensive word tumbled over his lips, Dylan looked around for a deep, dark hole to crawl into and needed Dr Mason to remove the size-11 foot firmly lodged in his mouth. Terri almost gave birth to a second cow after that verbal cannonball fired out of Dylan's mouth, but Lorraine was unfazed by it all and, after a brief yet deafening silence, she adroitly sidestepped the clumsy question by joking, "Of course I'm a hooker; how else do you think I can afford the annual dues here?"

After the laughter died down, Terri leaned in close to Mr Suave and whispered, "Why didn't you ask her how old she was too?"

"I, um, didn't have the chance."

"If you, um, had the chance, would you ask her how much she weighed as well?"

"No, I would've limited it to just her profession, nothing else."

"My mother was right; I married an idiot."

Dylan was on fire and played the round of his life, which confirmed the porridge hypothesis because a blue moon came and went three months earlier. Standing over a one-foot putt on the eighteenth green to shoot a final score of 99, Dylan was certain he could drain the easiest putt in the world with his eyes closed.

The game of golf is akin to a beautiful lady who shamelessly flirts with a man and then strolls away leaving him high and dry, alone with his thoughts and devastated by disappointment. Surging with confidence, Dylan addressed the ball, took a gentle stroke and watched in horror as the putt did a 360-degree horseshoe around the cup only to end up exactly where it started; history and his dream of bettering the 100-stroke threshold would have to wait another day.

After the golf tournament ended, liquor flowed and a buffet of comfort food was there for the taking and while helping herself to a plateful of chicken wings, Terri spotted Juliet Carfano, her lifelong arch-nemesis, standing off to the side. Dylan noticed the same thing and leaped into action to prevent an encore performance of the 'Toys R Us Incident' by blocking Terri's path to Juliet. The seeds of discord were sown twelve months earlier at Terri's high school reunion that culminated with Terri doing a little time in the slammer.

Born two days apart and growing up in the same neighborhood, Terri and Juliet plain didn't like each other since they were old enough to be consumed by blind hatred and raging jealousy. As the high school seniors blossomed into young women, Juliet took the animosity to a new level by stealing Terri's boyfriend.

Women tend to remember things like that—forever—and the thought of Juliet swooping in to lure Terri's man away was seared into her memory like a cattle brand. The archenemies traveled in different circles and never had any contact after high school until members of their graduating class organized a reunion fifteen years after-the-fact. Terri was the first to RSVP with visions of settling an old score while serving Juliet a heaping, ice-cold dish of revenge and circled that day on her calendar anxious to pay back the worst person ever born.

While Terri primped and preened getting ready for the event, Dylan threw caution to the wind and teased his better half hoping to lighten the mood but instead awakened a grumpy, hibernating bear: "You've made some terrible decisions in the past, but attending the reunion takes the cake. What are you going to do... murder Juliet and bury her in the woods?"

"The thought crossed my mind... soooooo, exactly what other 'terrible decisions' have I ever made?"

"For starters, you married me."

"A choice I've come to regret more and more with every passing day. What else ya' got, tough guy?"

Even though he should've known better, Dylan continued to charge directly into the line of fire and he reminded Terri of the time she streaked across Quinnipiac

University's campus on a particularly frigid day, which resulted in a minor case of frostbite—on her backside.

Terri pursed her lips and had a look in her eye that would frighten Navy SEALs as she informed Dylan there were mitigating factors leading up to the wintertime sprint, blaming sorority hazing as the culprit. Terri then asked one of those questions women ask men when they're spoiling for a fight and requested Dylan's opinion about whether a certain anatomical feature of hers still looked good after all these years. Any married man with even one functioning brain cell knows a question like that demands only one answer or he'll be pitching a tent over the couch for an unspecified period of time.

Dylan hesitated a bit knowing full well the answer he'd provide might be the difference between life and death, and smartly remarked that on a one to ten scale Terri's magnificent body part was, "an eleven, going on twelve."

Terri didn't mince words and hoped Juliet had a wretched life filled with misfortune, misery and despair, and would be virtually unrecognizable after pouring on the pounds. After delivering those rays of sunshine to Dylan, Terri grabbed his arm and headed for the reunion.

On a balmy summer evening, former classmates shared a laugh about the trials and tribulations of navigating the stormy waters known as high school—everyone except Terri, of course. As Terri waited in line to order a drink, she sensed a presence that raised the hair on the back of her neck and as she turned around, there stood Juliet a few feet away.

There she is, Terri thought—the harlot, the man-stealing wench—and Juliet flashed one of those cat-swallowed-the-canary smiles Terri's way that lit the fuse.

The blood rivals circled each other ending up face-to-face with Terri giving Juliet the once-over stink eye and through tightly clenched teeth Terri meowed, "I love your dress; did you buy it at Omar the Tentmaker's closeout sale?"

"Always with a big mouth; I hope Thigh Master offers a money back guarantee because, honey, it ain't workin' for you."

"Speaking of big, how many hours did it take to shoehorn your half-acre ass into that outfit?"

Dylan was on high alert knowing that even the slightest spark between Terri and Juliet could disintegrate into a DEFCON 1, Earth-consuming nuclear conflict in a matter of seconds. Keeping a close eye on Terri, Dylan intervened to defuse the situation and gently guided Terri away before she started a folding-chair-throwing, steel cage death match. The rest of the evening went off without any more confrontations but there was tension in the air, unresolved tension, and it was only a matter of time before Terri and Juliet met on the battlefield again.

Summer turned to fall and a crisp autumn chill gave way to frigid winter temperatures heralding the arrival of Christmas. The 'must-have' gift for the holiday season was a doll and Terri headed to Toys R Us to purchase one for her niece. Nary one parking space was available on this mid-December afternoon and along with several other impatient, borderline berserk Christmas shoppers, Terri circled the lot waiting for a space to clear ready to pounce on it like a mongoose on a cobra.

Terri noticed a car pull out two rows over but someone else saw the same thing: it was none other than Juliet. The arch-nemeses made eye contact and then stepped on the gas racing toward the empty space rapidly approaching from opposite directions; turning into the space at the same time the vehicles' front bumpers came to a pyramid point as both drivers tried to finesse each other out of the way.

Which spineless coward would flinch first? The combatants honked their horns, waved at each other with middle fingers held high and repeated the insults from the reunion—adding colorful comments for clarity. Unbowed and standing tall, neither lady budged an inch.

Death took a holiday when another car pulled out one row over and Terri slammed it into reverse while directing a few un-ladylike words and hand gestures toward Juliet, who responded in similar fashion with sailor-blushing language and a stray finger or two. Terri practically ran into the store while Juliet bided her time talking to someone on her cell phone but fate had a different plan: put Terri and Juliet on a collision course and let the chips fall where they may.

Juliet went to Toys R Us to purchase the same 'must-have' doll for a family member and in a spooky case of instant déjà vu both women entered the doll aisle from opposite ends but didn't notice each other right away, instead focusing on finding the doll in question. Just as Terri located the doll—the last one on the shelf—the hair on the back of her neck stood up again; Terri turned and was once again face-to-face with Jezebel.

Uh oh; it only took *one* look—Mr Match meet Mrs Gasoline.

Unleashing bloodcurdling screams that could awaken the dearly departed, Terri and Juliet simultaneously lunged for the doll with each getting a hand on the package at the same time. They grappled together falling to the floor in an eye-gouging, hair-pulling, roll-around-on-the-floor catfight while threatening each other with particularly painful forms of death and destruction. Moments later store security arrived on scene, separated the mighty soldiers and waited for the police to arrive who arrested the ladies for disturbing the peace.

Dylan's afternoon of quiet solitude was rudely interrupted by Officer Radford who kindly requested Dylan's presence at police headquarters to post bail for his hardened criminal of a wife. After being told why Terri got arrested, Dylan lit into her, his turn not to mince words and gave Terri a tongue-lashing suggesting her behavior would even embarrass a two-year old throwing a temper tantrum. Terri's face was scratched but Juliet got the worst of it:

"You gave Juliet a black eye… and broke her wrist?" Dylan asked in disbelief as he perused the official police report.

"No, no, no; her wrist isn't broken, it's only sprained and *I* didn't give her a black eye; as we fell to the ground, Juliet's face just happened to land on my fist."

"I married Rambo… you do know the doll has a higher IQ than the two of you combined, right?"

"I graduated with a higher GPA than that dumb bitch."

"Says the woman in police custody; OK Rambo, it's time to go home."

Terri had a police record and proudly carried that as a badge of honor for the rest of her life, keeping a copy of her mug shot for posterity's sake and as a reminder about the afternoon she served up a healthy dose of Karma to a hated enemy.

As the grandkids reached double-digits in age, Rebecca's body betrayed her and she became frail, almost brittle, barely able to care for herself. Dylan had a difficult choice to make: he didn't have the time to assist Rebecca with her day-to-day needs but she couldn't live under his roof either because there was a lack of space in the modest Cape—if Rebecca moved in, building an addition to the home would be required. Dylan could purchase another home that came with an in-law apartment, but he had no desire to move from the bucolic, tranquil beauty of Granite Bay and neither would Terri.

A viable option would be placing Rebecca in an assisted living facility where she could be monitored day and night, as well as the added benefit of keeping Terri and Rebecca at arm's length, just in case their relationship reverted to form. Seaside Manor seemed to be the perfect answer: located in Branford, Seaside had a reputation of providing top-notch care by an experienced medical staff. The waterfront facility treated residents to exquisite vistas of Branford's undulating, granite-lined shore and it just didn't get any better than living here, period.

Dylan was proactive and scheduled a meeting with Ashley, the Intake Coordinator at Seaside Manor, but first spoke to Mom trying to persuade her that residing in an assisted living facility was the best of both worlds. Rebecca's reaction was swift and predictable, and she played the guilt card of motherly disappointment to the hilt.

She bitterly complained that Dylan was cruel and heartless willing to abandon his own mother, acting as if she took a dagger to the heart and said she'd be better off if Dylan dumped her in front of a Greyhound bus station with a suitcase and one-way ticket to the boondocks of Kankakee, Illinois. Dylan stood fast in the face of withering adversity and told Rebecca of his impending meeting at Seaside Manor and then deserted his wounded, mopey mother to meet with Ashley.

Dylan thanked Ashley for taking the meeting and deadpanned that his mother needed the assistance provided by Seaside Manor's skilled healthcare professionals especially those with a background in treating mental illness.

That's the understatement of the millennium, Ashley thought as she put the kibosh on Rebecca's admission explaining there were no apartments available at the moment. Dylan was shocked; he spoke to Ashley only two hours earlier and asked what happened in the interim; Ashley nervously moved papers around on her desk and with no conviction at all offered the weak excuse that things move fast in this business and circumstances changed.

Dylan smelled a rat—a conniving rodent named Rebecca. "When did she call and how many idle threats did she make?"

"She?"

"You know perfectly well who I mean: my mother, Rebecca."

"Oh, that she. Well, a few moments before you arrived."

"And?"

"There was nothing idle about her threats."

Rebecca promised to sue Seaside Manor, Ashley and anyone else she could think of for a figure north of one hundred gazillion dollars if she was admitted to the facility;

Dylan headed home not looking forward to breaking the news to Terri that Rebecca would be spending her remaining days at Chateau Steele in Granite Bay after an addition was built.

Dylan reflected for a moment about where it all went wrong and took a walk down memory lane to his childhood when livin' was easy, Dad was still alive and Mom wasn't a stark, raving lunatic. He recalled those glorious times when a blizzard canceled school and he'd spend the day hurtling down snow-covered hills on his Flexible Flyer, the exhilaration of speed overcoming the fear of crashing head-first into a snowbank. His face would get beet red, scraped raw by icy snowflakes and needles of sleet but that didn't matter: anything was better than being in school.

Dylan arrived home with a dazed look splashed all over his face and Terri quipped that she hadn't seen Dylan look this glassy-eyed since last New Years' Eve but Dylan gave her nuthin'—not even a little smile—and just stood there measuring his words. He asked Terri what her definition of really, really, really bad news was and she knew right away Rebecca wasn't moving into Seaside Manor.

Terri gazed despondently toward the heavens and prayed for divine intervention: "Dear God: I know we haven't spoken in a while—all right, you got me; this is the first time… which is understandable because why would God speak with a mortal sinner who was *this close* to committing murder—twice? But let's be reasonable, shall we? I only *thought* about killing Rebecca and Juliet's a jerk who got off easy, so will you please look the other way and give me a pass this one time? The reason I reached out is to ask you to force Ashley to change her mind—I'm begging you on bended knee. Thanks for taking care of that, *mucho apreciado.*"

Typically, God isn't in the habit of descending from his heavenly perch to strong-arm Intake Coordinators to do something they shouldn't and He rightly remained impartial. It took nine months for the addition to be completed and sometimes the anticipation of coping with a bad situation is worse than the actual event and having Rebecca move to Granite Bay wasn't nearly as disastrous as Terri thought it would be.

Rebecca didn't fall back into bad habits and for the most part she was on her best behavior but several years later Rebecca succumbed to the vagaries of her failing health, laid to rest next to her cherished husband at Saint Agnes cemetery.

As the minister's final words faded into silence and Rebecca's casket slid smoothly into her grave, Terri was sad… sad for Dylan, sad for her children who were heartbroken at Rebecca's passing, but Terri wasn't that sad for herself; some things you just don't get over and "Plan B" was one of those things.

Sam and Amy were in high school when Rebecca passed and they struggled to cope with the loss, especially Amy who developed a special bond with grandma. Emotional upheaval, raging hormones and a romantic rival buzzing around Amy's boyfriend pushed Amy to the edge and she protected her turf, the Marquis of Queensberry rules be damned.

Amy didn't suffer fools for long and, like mother, like daughter, Amy had a predilection for grim retaliation if someone got on her bad side—and that someone was a man-stealing hussy named Lauren. Amy contemplated the best way to permanently remove Lauren from life's equation in the most horrific way possible and not end up in the big house—dark woods... shovel to the face... into a lime-filled hole—but wisely chose freedom over six-by-nine accommodations with steel bars.

Instead, Amy confronted the relationship wrecker and instructed Lauren to keep her paws off Amy's man, or else. Amy gave Lauren one of those *slooooooww*, up-and-down once-overs and noted if Lauren was launched into outer space, her giant ass would cause a total eclipse of the Sun.

Lauren responded in kind remarking that even daily liposuction treatments wouldn't help Amy's thunder-thigh problem and before you could say "let's get ready to rumble!" both ladies were on the ground auditioning for roles in the World Wrestling Federation. Over dinner later that evening, Terri asked Amy about her day at school.

"It was OK; I got an 'A' on a history test, got invited to a party this weekend and..." Amy's voice trailed off.

"And what, dear?"

"Well... I got suspended from school for giving Lauren a black eye and separating her shoulder, but that's not true—it's only a sprain. And *I* didn't give her a black eye—she got it after losing her balance and then fell face-first into my fist."

"Lauren... the tramp muscling in on your boyfriend... that Lauren?"

"That's the tramp."

Terri flashed a broad smile, giving Amy a big hug and then regaled her daughter with the details of the 'Toys R Us Incident.' After Terri broke out the badge-of-honor mug shot, Amy developed a new-found respect for mom; once a healer of the sick, now Terri was a badass mother for the ages, taking no names and leaving no one standing who dared get in her way.

When Sam was in high school, he chose not to seriously injure his fellow students and instead focused on applying to colleges and, even more important, getting his driver's license. Dylan made Sam wait until senior year and hired Phil's Driving School to teach Sam the fine points of maneuvering two tons of metal and rubber over highways, byways and driveways. Phil's had a sterling reputation of teaching teenagers how to avoid ricocheting off oncoming traffic while steering clear of those pesky pedestrians in crosswalks and Dylan gladly paid professionals to teach Sam how to be a safe, courteous driver.

Nicknamed 'Bouffy,' short for the ginormous bouffant perched on top of her head, Marie Lombardi was assigned as Sam's instructor and she didn't waste time putting her students to the test. Sam survived the first driving lesson without incident but knew he was in trouble taking lesson number two when Bouffy asked if he was ready to become a man.

Bouffy ordered Sam to drive into New Haven... on a highway... over a bridge... on a rainy, windy day. Interstate 95 from Branford into New Haven is six lanes of terror-filled, high-speed blacktop and anyone who drives that stretch needs to put his affairs in order before leaving home. Sam cautiously crawled up an entrance ramp to merge with traffic—too cautiously—and Bouffy took over the controls to safely blend with vehicles whizzing past them at seventy miles per hour. Bouffy directed a few words in Italian toward a truck driver—and it didn't sound like she invited him over for afternoon tea—because Bouffy had to swerve out of the way to prevent getting crushed by an eighteen-wheeler driven by a pill-popping maniac with no regard for human life.

While en route to the big city, Bouffy called her sister and cryptically asked if the package was ready; Sam expressed concern as to what the package contained but Bouffy swatted away his worries and told him to "fuhget about it." The complexities of Italian slang aside, Sam didn't have time to fuhget the unfuhgettable because Bouffy barked out directions guiding Sam through the city streets of New Haven to her sister's home.

Bouffy ran in and moments later emerged holding a shoe box; Sam's imagination ran wild and he wondered what was inside: a severed finger and ransom note, stacks of freshly laundered Benjamins or was it simply what it seemed to be—a pair of shoes. Bouffy instructed Sam to head back to the barn but there was one more stop to make before the barn doors closed for the night—delivering the shoe box to Rose, another sister who lived in the neighboring town of East Haven.

The East Haven wing of the Lombardi family were practicing Catholics who went forth and multiplied at a breathtaking rate with Petey, Mikey, Pauley and Marie all under the age of eight and prime examples of why the rhythm method of birth control is an utter waste of time. Explaining she'd be a while, Bouffy invited Sam inside and he had no idea he was about to experience something more terrifying than driving on an Interstate, over a bridge, in a blinding rainstorm: dinner hour in an Italian household.

As Sam stepped foot into the kitchen, there was screaming and yelling the likes of which he'd never heard before: this wasn't dinner, it was a smorgasbord—of bedlam, mayhem and pandemonium. Out of the corner of his eye, Sam saw a UFO hurtling toward him and he hit the deck just in time as a meatball zipped over his head.

Four out-of-control children engaged in an all-out food fight as Petey dumped a plate of spaghetti on Mikey's head and then Mikey mushed Pauley's face with a few strands of pasta. Not to be outdone, Marie rinsed off Mikey's head with a glass of soda, and fired another beef-y artillery round at Sam but missed by a wide margin.

The youngins' merrily pummeled one another while Rose blissfully ignored the turmoil raging all around and casually went about her business acting as if nothing was wrong. "Fuhget about it!" Rose squealed with joy as she opened the shoe box and removed... a spiffy pair of Jimmy Choos.

More and more confused, Sam considered hiring an Italian language expert to first translate *faccia di culo*, the words of endearment Bouffy shared with the truck driver, as well as the flexible meaning of fuhget about it. A few moments later Bouffy ushered Sam out the door to complete the final leg of their journey and he was thrilled to exit the house of horrors with all his limbs and vital organs still intact.

After arriving home, a concerned Dylan asked his visibly shell-shocked child how driving lesson number two went; "Fuhget about it," Sam replied with a weak smile and left dad hangin' without a translation and two months later Sam began roaming Branford's streets as a licensed driver.

Known as the Three Musketeers, Sam and two friends were inseparable during high school and stalked the hallways of Branford High believing they were the most magnificent *Homo sapiens* to ever grace the universe. Gods and goddesses on Mount Olympus couldn't help but weep in the presence of Musketeer greatness but Musketeer parents, well, let's just say they saw things differently.

Even though Zeus, Apollo and Aphrodite shed no tears, exasperated, at-their-wits-end Musketeer parents did, sick and tired of being sick and tired of youthful arrogance and smart-ass back talk. Those same parents didn't view the Musketeers as three of the world's seven wonders and showed admirable self-control coping with insufferable children without going to the woodshed to impart some much-needed personality adjustment.

Terri devised a plan to give the Musketeer elders a much-needed break from mouthy demi-gods and arranged a conference call among Musketeer moms seeking permission to ship out their offspring to spend Saturday night at the home of Terri's brother.

Terri: "After a little arm twisting, my brother agreed to let the Musketeers stay overnight at his house in Salisbury. Are you OK with that?"

Musketeer Mom #2 [crying tears of joy]: "Just one night? How about two... weeks?"

Musketeer Mom #3 [weeping in ecstasy]: "I'll pony up five grand right now, no questions asked, for a month."

Musketeer Mom #2 [still crying]: "Is your brother open to the idea of adoption? I'll sign the papers tomorrow."

Terri: "No dice; I already asked and got a hard 'no.'"

Uncle Mike lived in the far northwestern corner of Connecticut smack dab in the rolling hills of the southern Berkshire Mountains. He wasn't married and owned a sprawling, four-bedroom log cabin with more than enough room to accommodate the Musketeers and he reluctantly agreed to let them stay overnight—only doing so because Terri blackmailed her brother about a particularly humiliating event that he wanted to forget about but couldn't, thanks to Terri's threats to reveal a secret only the two siblings shared.

It all went sideways for Mike when in a tequila-fueled fog he tried to entice a woman to come home with him but the woman was... a man. Terri casually mentioned—again, for the billionth time—that for most guys an Adam's apple the size of a peach pit would've been a dead giveaway and threatened to go public with the information if Mike didn't allow the Musketeers into his home.

Dylan's father was a classic car buff and after dad passed away, Dylan took possession of a 1960 Corvair convertible. Dylan let the Musketeers take the Suntan Copper-colored vehicle to Salisbury knowing full well the

Corvair was barely safe enough to drive across the street, let alone make a 160-mile round trip that was 159.9 miles too far for this the bucket of bolts to travel.

Dylan hoped the cocky trio would get taken down a peg or two if they got stranded ten miles west of nowhere because Corvairs were anything but reliable. The rust-covered vehicle had four tires worn down to the cords and almost 100,000 miles under its dilapidated belt, and it was highly unlikely the car would survive the journey.

Unchaperoned for the first time ever, the Musketeers Jack Kerouac-ed over Connecticut's twisty back roads and it was an unsolvable mystery how the barely functional vehicle made it to Salisbury without disintegrating into a fine dust but fortunately, it did. The Musketeers spent the night staying up until the wee hours having a deep, deeper, deepest conversation about the meaning of life, once again reaffirming their awe-inspiring abilities to grasp complicated subject matter mere mortals could never understand.

After Uncle Mike fed the Musketeers a mid-morning breakfast of pancakes and bacon, he unceremoniously shoved the trio out the door; he called Terri and told his mean-spirited sister to just go ahead and blow the lid off the secret because there was no way he'd allow the Musketeers to ever darken his door again.

The ride home put the pants-wetting fear of Zeus into the latest inductees to the Mount Olympus Hall of Fame because the Corvair violently shuddered at speeds over fifty miles per hour with constant tapping noises coming from the engine. Loud snaps, pops and crunching metallic sounds added to the Musketeers' anxiety level as they came to the inescapable conclusion that life is short and they were likely to die.

It was another unsolvable mystery how the Musketeers safely arrived in Granite Bay but fortunately, three excruciatingly long hours later, they did. Sam pulled the death trap into his driveway and wasting no time at all, one Musketeer leaped out of the car while it was still moving, fell to the ground and yelled, "Land!" Moments after the Musketeers all safely exited the vehicle, the rust bucket creaked, groaned and collapsed onto its frame, flattening all four tires while sending dirt and debris in every direction: the Corvair was deader than the Ford Edsel and would never see the open road again.

"It's a shame, Dylan," Terri sighed as the elder Steeles gazed out the living room window witnessing the drama and carnage happening right before their eyes.

"I agree; I planned on restoring that car."

"No, what I meant is that it's too bad the Musketeers found their way back home; they must've left a trail of breadcrumbs."

"Yeah… just when I got used to Sam not being here…"

"There is one silver lining, though."

"I'm listening."

"Only seven months and five days before Sam heads off to college."

"That is good news… so, what's for lunch?"

Where did the time go? Sam and Amy flew the coop starting lives of their own and after the empty nesters were retired for a few years, circumstances beyond their control changed everything: falling stock markets drove a stake through the heart of their finances. Money disappeared faster than cake and ice cream at a birthday party and faced with a financial apocalypse, the Steeles had no choice but to re-join the ranks of the employed needing at least part-time jobs to make ends meet.

Terri had no problem finding work; there were plenty of opportunities for a person with her clinical abilities and Dylan could've found work with his background in accounting but he didn't want to crunch numbers any more and changed things up by following his creative passion.

A part-time bookseller position opened up at Barnes & Noble and given Dylan's love of American literature as well as being a published author, the job seemed like a perfect fit. Dylan couldn't hit the 'Send' button fast enough to email his resume and Denise Wellington, Barnes & Noble's Human Resources Manager, responded within an hour scheduling an interview for the next day.

Anxious about going through the job-interview wringer for the first time in decades, Dylan accentuated the positive knowing his experience matched up well with the job responsibilities. *I can do this*, Dylan thought; piece of cake.

What is it with the Steele family and those famous last words?

Dylan entered Denise's office and stopped dead in his tracks because she was decked out in an all-black outfit that an executioner might wear during the Middle Ages. She stood bolt upright, walking with an awkward, stilted gait and her hair was pulled back so tightly that it looked painful; something was off about Denise—way, way, off—and Dylan hoped she'd at least have the courtesy to sharpen the blade before slicing him into bite -size pieces as he thought, *goodbye everybody; it's been a good run—see ya' on the other side.*

Denise had a script and followed it to the letter interrogating Dylan like he was a suspect in a murder investigation and posed befuddling questions irrelevant to the bookseller position. Already fidgety with Denise's off-putting style, Dylan squirmed even more after she fired a warning shot across the bow: "First question: what are three things you learned about yourself in your first job?"

Dylan's mind raced: I can barely remember what I ate for breakfast and Denise wants me to remember not one, not two but three life-changing epiphanies I had bagging groceries in a supermarket? And not for nothing, who in their right mind goes through life keeping a list of 'Things I Learned about Myself'—is that something you scotch tape to the refrigerator so you don't forget? Hmmm, let's see; I did just learn one thing: dumb questions annoy me.

Exercising considerable self-restraint, Dylan stopped just short of blurting out a wildly inappropriate response about the time he and a nubile cashier shared a few passionate moments in the market's backroom, got caught red-handed and fired on the spot. Instead, with tongue firmly planted in cheek, Dylan mentioned three things he learned the hard way when he was a teenager: 1) NEVER ask a slightly overweight woman "when's the baby due?" 2) there ain't no walking back from number one 3) don't try to apologize; it just makes things worse.

Denise grimaced and made a mark on the checklist she held in her hand. "I understand," she replied unemotionally. "Next question: if you could be any animal, which one would you be?"

Really, Dylan thought, *the animal question?* He hemmed and hawed pondering the best way to respond to an outdated, lame technique intended to draw out a candidate's true colors by comparing the applicant's personality to the animal he or she chose to emulate such as German Shepherd = strong and loyal, or Golden Retriever = kind and gentle.

Getting more and more annoyed with Denise's mystifying questions, Dylan *almost* launched a missile sitting there on the tip of his tongue: You want animal, honey? Fine; how's this? Right now, I want to be a skunk because I'd raise my tail and give you a faceful. How's that for animal, huh? Huh?

Dylan held his tongue and after a moment of cautious reflection quipped, "Lions, tigers and bears; oh my!" Denise sat there impassively not responding at all and then Dylan added, "Dorothy? *The Wizard of Oz?* I was kidding."

"Right," Denise said as she checked off another box on the list.

Denise never cracked a smile the entire time and she blindly forged ahead asking another head-scratcher: "Next question: how many planes are flying in the skies over the United States right now?"

Confronted by another senseless question that had no bearing on the job at hand, Dylan lost control of his self-control and wisecracked, "Hopefully all of them… except for the one taking my ex-wife to the vacation home she got in the divorce."

Denise almost let a tiny smile slip as her lips curled up ever so slightly—almost. Reeling from Denise's bizarre questions, Dylan wondered what other techniques she'd employ trying to squeeeeeeeeeeeeeeeeeeze information out of him: jamming bamboo shoots under his fingernails or forcing him to walk barefoot across a bed of hot coals were distinct possibilities. Or one followed by the other. Or worse.

Dylan didn't have to wait long for an answer. Denise surpassed all expectations, unable to grasp the sheer irony of asking Dylan where he saw himself ten years into the future—perhaps the most dimwitted question anyone could ask a sixty-eight-year-old man with diabetes, a bad attitude and nothing left to lose. Dylan gazed forlornly toward the heavens and now it was his turn to pray for divine intervention.

"Dear God, I know we haven't chatted in a while—OK, you got me, we've never chatted at all... which is understandable based on the op-ed piece about the Catholic Church I contributed to the *Argus*, Wesleyan University's campus newspaper. Hatchet job is a bit strong but come on; you've got a sense of humor, right? It was a joke, so be the bigger man and let bygones be bygones, and then we can all move on from this misunderstanding. The reason I made contact is to ask you to threaten Denise with a life in Hell if she doesn't stop acting like a meathead—I'm pleading with you on my hands and knees. Thanks for your assistance; it's greatly appreciated."

Unfortunately, God had a long memory, a broken funny bone and turned a deaf ear to the heartfelt plea leaving Dylan dangling over the edge of a cliff by his fingernails. Having just been asked where he'll be at age seventy-eight Dylan thought, *does "ashes to ashes and dust to dust" ring a bell?* Secure in the knowledge the answer he was about to provide would preclude him from ever being hired and with a look of certain doom etched across his face Dylan answered, "On my deathbed in a diabetic coma."

Expressionless as always, Denise checked off the final box on the list and abruptly stood up. Lying through her teeth and without a shred of sincerity, Denise thanked Dylan for his time, said she'd be in touch and pointed him toward the door. Needless to say, Dylan had no shot at being hired and he arrived home with yet another dazed, glassy-eyed look splashed across his face. Terri knew right away Barnes & Noble didn't work out and commiserated with her better half:

"I take it the interview didn't go well; sorry."

"Passing a kidney stone the size of a bowling ball would've been less agonizing... or sticking my honey-covered hand into a nest of angry hornets... or being the main course for a tribe of cannibalistic headhunters..."

"All right, already; I get it: it was bad—really, really, really bad. What happened?"

"Nothing... everything; if you're ever asked to rattle off three things you learned about yourself in your first job, head for the hills—your life is over."

Dylan wallowed in misery but not for long because the next day there were televised reports showing none other than Denise Wellington, aka Mistress Medieval, being led away in handcuffs from a bondage and discipline house of ill repute called The Whipping Post.

Humorless Human Resources Manager by day and flagellating, heel-grinding, pain-inflicting Dominatrix by night—a distinction without even one sliver of difference—Mistress Medieval enthusiastically beat, abused and tormented her willing clientele until they whimpered to make it stop; at least with Denise's day job, the willing clientele walked out the door humiliated and psychologically damaged, not needing medical attention or stitches.

In the aftermath of her arrest Denise played the victim card claiming a prescription mix-up caused her to behave out of character but the powers that be weren't buying it. Barnes & Noble gave Denise her walking papers and now it would be her turn to answer uncomfortable interview questions describing her work experience at The Whipping Post.

A new Human Resources Manager took over shortly thereafter and realized Dylan drew the short straw with Denise. The new boss scheduled another interview and didn't ask Dylan foolish questions especially one about gazing into a crystal ball to predict the future.

Dylan got the job.

Terri and Dylan worked for a few years to keep the flow flowing and after their investments rebounded courtesy of a bull market, they opted for full retirement. Remarkably spry for their age, the elder Steeles continued to play golf on occasion and Terri kept purchasing Meissen pieces, filling up a second china closet with valuable porcelain. Terri and Dylan lived a long, loving life together and became grandparents to Stella, Zach and Ellie, and despite the strong desire to spend time with adorable grandchildren, Terri never hovered and smothered, had demons cast off or took a header down a flight of stairs. It's the little things in life that make all the difference.